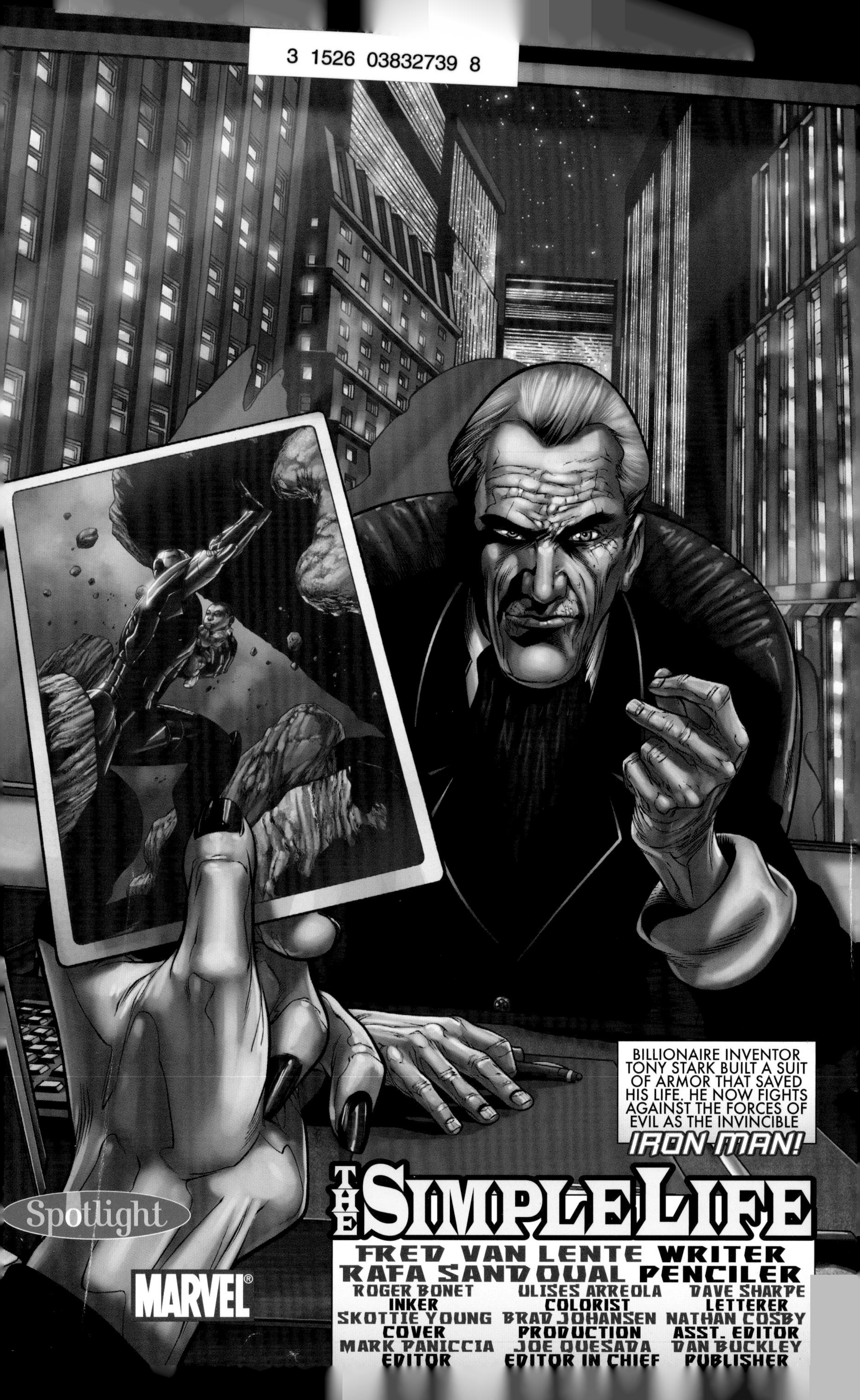

BILLIONAIRE INVENTOR TONY STARK BUILT A SUIT OF ARMOR THAT SAVED HIS LIFE. HE NOW FIGHTS AGAINST THE FORCES OF EVIL AS THE INVINCIBLE
IRON MAN!
THE SIMPLE LIFE
FRED VAN LENTE WRITER
RAFA SANDOVAL PENCILER
ROGER BONET INKER
ULISES ARREOLA COLORIST
DAVE SHARPE LETTERER
SKOTTIE YOUNG COVER
BRAD JOHANSEN PRODUCTION
NATHAN COSBY ASST. EDITOR
MARK PANICCIA EDITOR
JOE QUESADA EDITOR IN CHIEF
DAN BUCKLEY PUBLISHER
Spotlight
MARVEL®

VISIT US AT
www.abdopublishing.com

Reinforced library bound edition published in 2009 by Spotlight, a division of the ABDO Group, 8000 West 78th Street, Edina, Minnesota 55439. Spotlight produces high-quality reinforced library bound editions for schools and libraries. Published by agreement with Marvel Characters, Inc.

Library of Congress Cataloging-in-Publication Data

Van Lente, Fred.
  The simple life / Fred Van Lente, writer ; Rafa Sandoval, penciler ; Roger Bonet, inker ; Ulises Arreola, colorist ; Dave Sharpe, letterer ; Skottie Young, cover. -- Reinforced library bound ed.
    p. cm. -- (Iron Man)
  "Marvel."
  ISBN 978-1-59961-592-9
  1. Graphic novels. [1. Graphic novels. 2. Superheroes--Fiction.] I. Sandoval, Rafa, ill. II. Title.
  PZ7.7.V26Si 2009
  741.5'973--dc22

                    2008033398

All Spotlight books have reinforced library bindings and are manufactured in the United States of America.

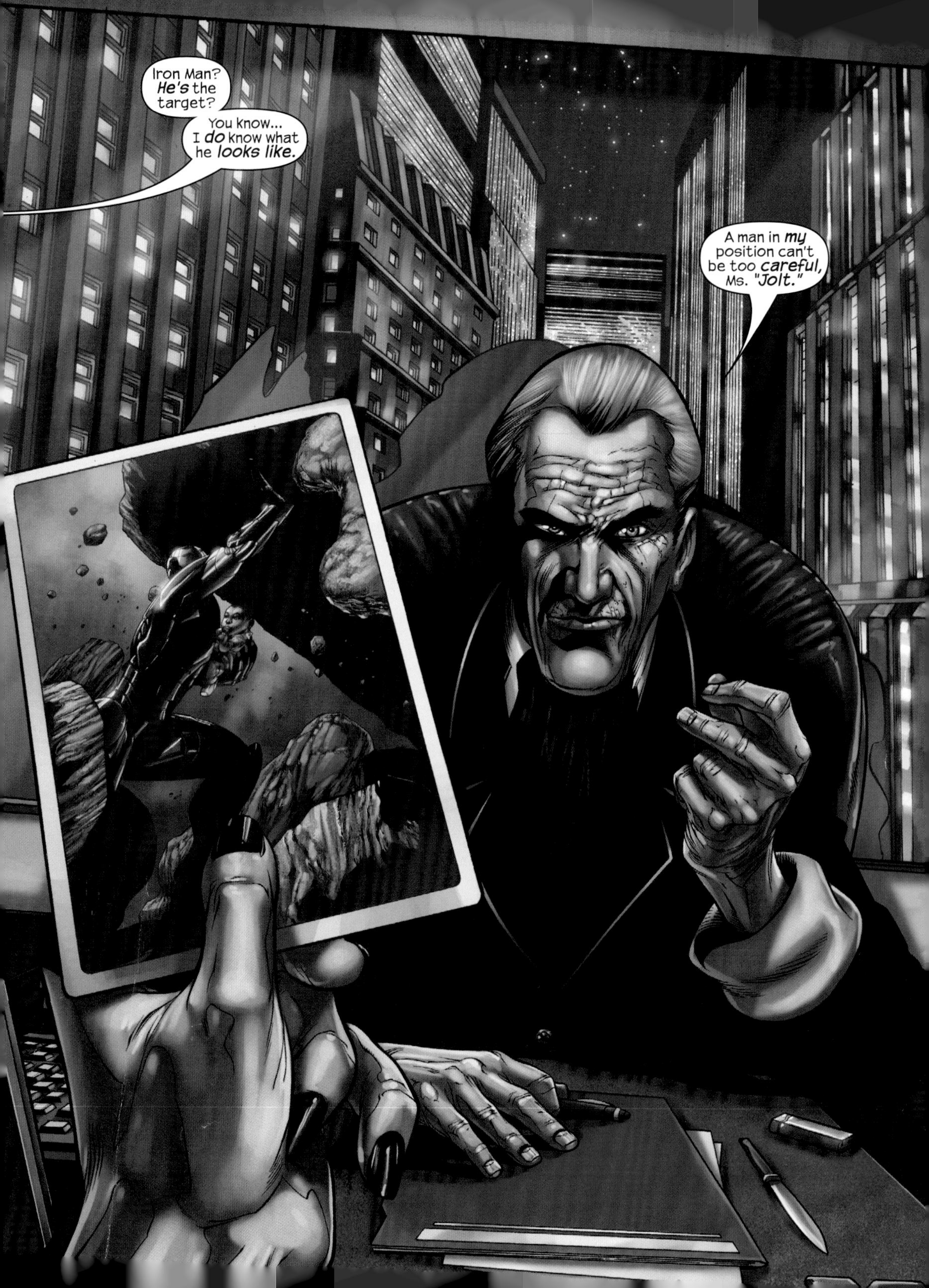
Iron Man? *He's* the target?
You know... I *do* know what he *looks like.*
A man in *my* position can't be too *careful,* Ms. "*Jolt.*"

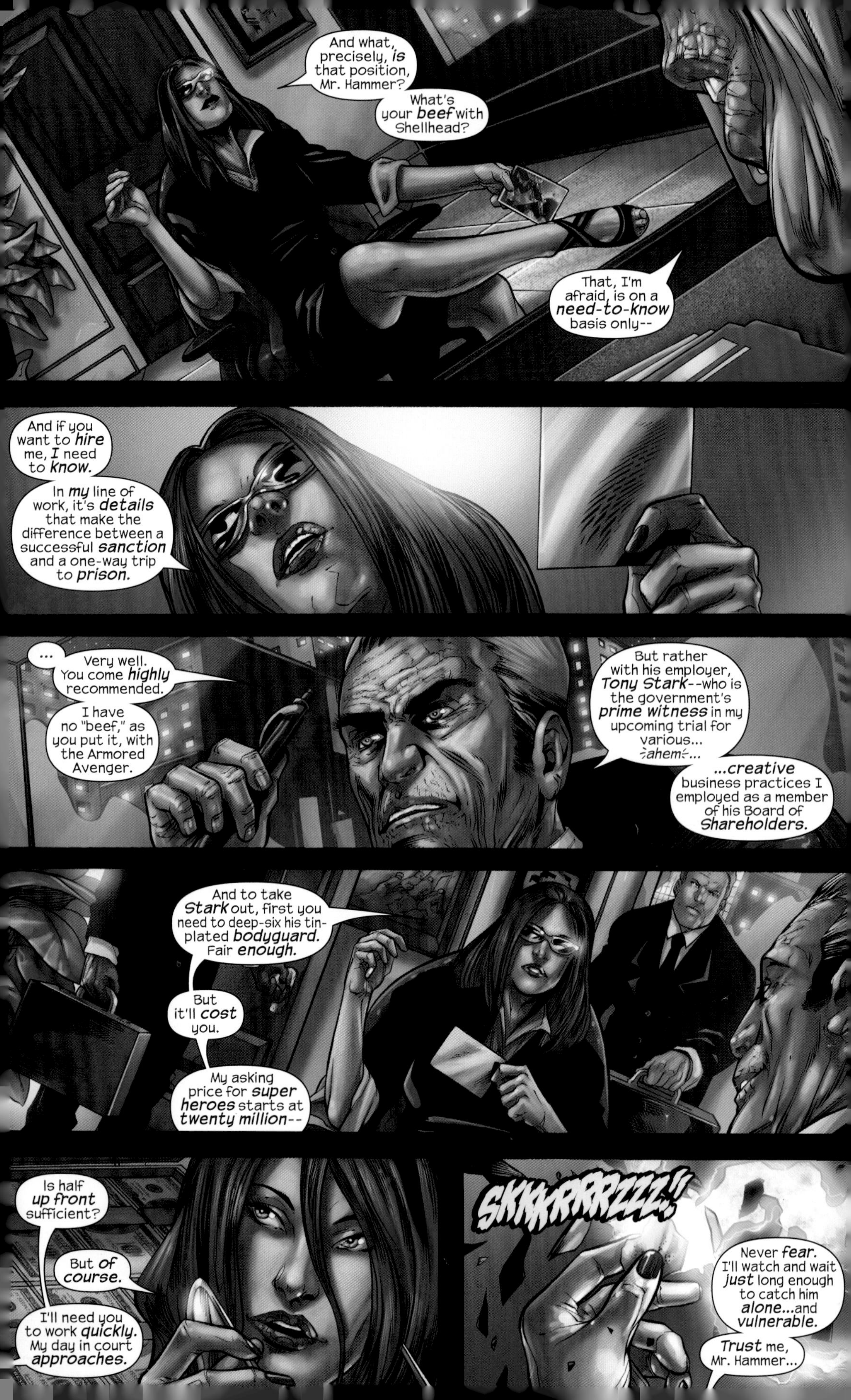
And what, precisely, is that position, Mr. Hammer?
What's your beef with Shellhead?
That, I'm afraid, is on a need-to-know basis only--
And if you want to hire me, I need to know.
In my line of work, it's details that make the difference between a successful sanction and a one-way trip to prison.
...
Very well. You come highly recommended.
I have no "beef," as you put it, with the Armored Avenger.
But rather with his employer, Tony Stark--who is the government's prime witness in my upcoming trial for various... ahem...
...creative business practices I employed as a member of his Board of Shareholders.
And to take Stark out, first you need to deep-six his tin-plated bodyguard. Fair enough.
But it'll cost you.
My asking price for super heroes starts at twenty million--
Is half up front sufficient?
But of course.
I'll need you to work quickly. My day in court approaches.
SKKKRRRZZZ!!
Never fear. I'll watch and wait just long enough to catch him alone...and vulnerable.
Trust me, Mr. Hammer...

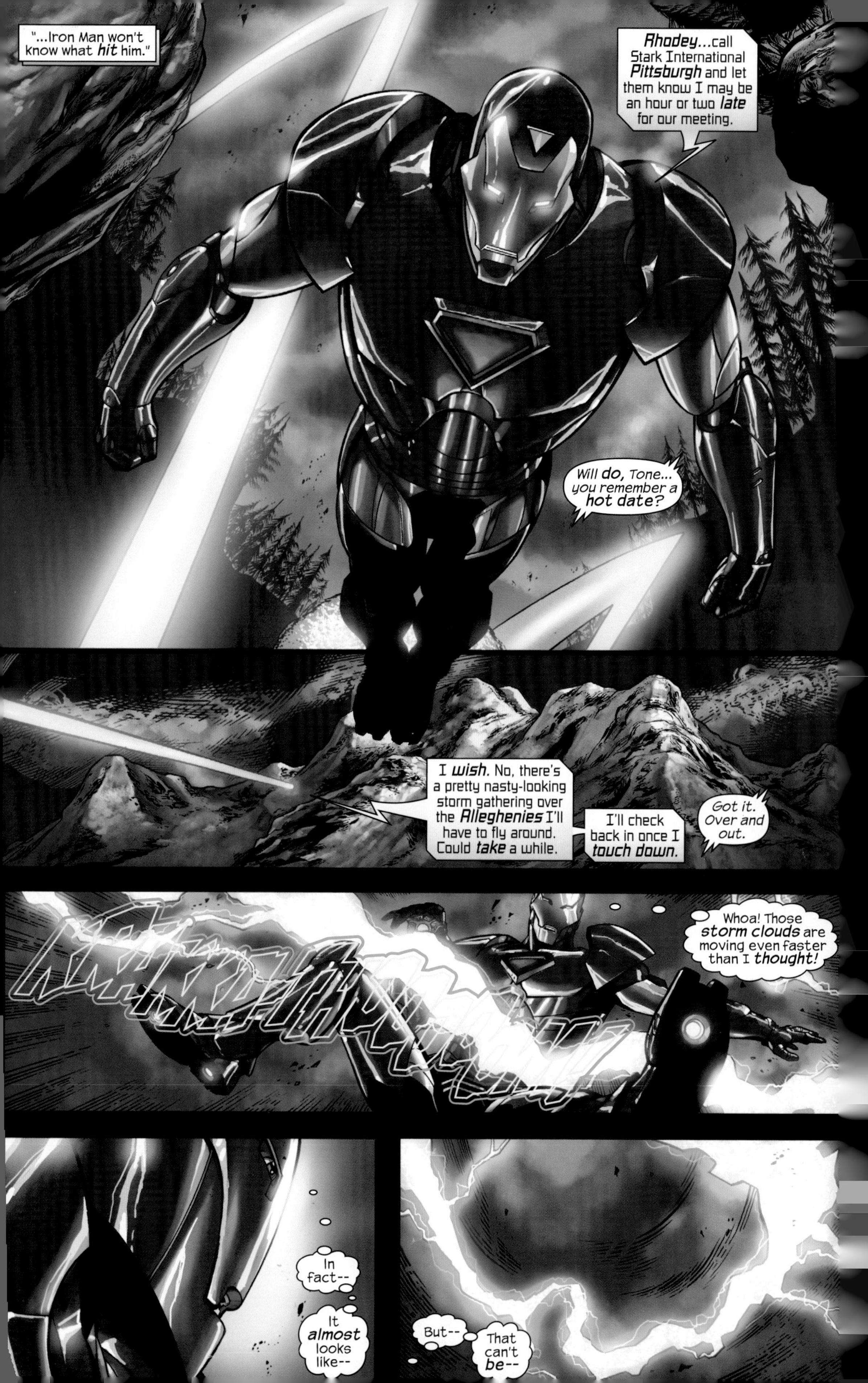
"...Iron Man won't know what *hit* him."
Rhodey...call Stark International *Pittsburgh* and let them know I may be an hour or two *late* for our meeting.
Will **do,** Tone... you remember a **hot date?**
I *wish*. No, there's a pretty nasty-looking storm gathering over the *Alleghenies* I'll have to fly around. Could *take* a while.
I'll check back in once I *touch down*.
Got it. Over and out.
Whoa! Those *storm clouds* are moving even faster than I *thought!*
In fact--
It *almost* looks like--
But--
That can't *be*--

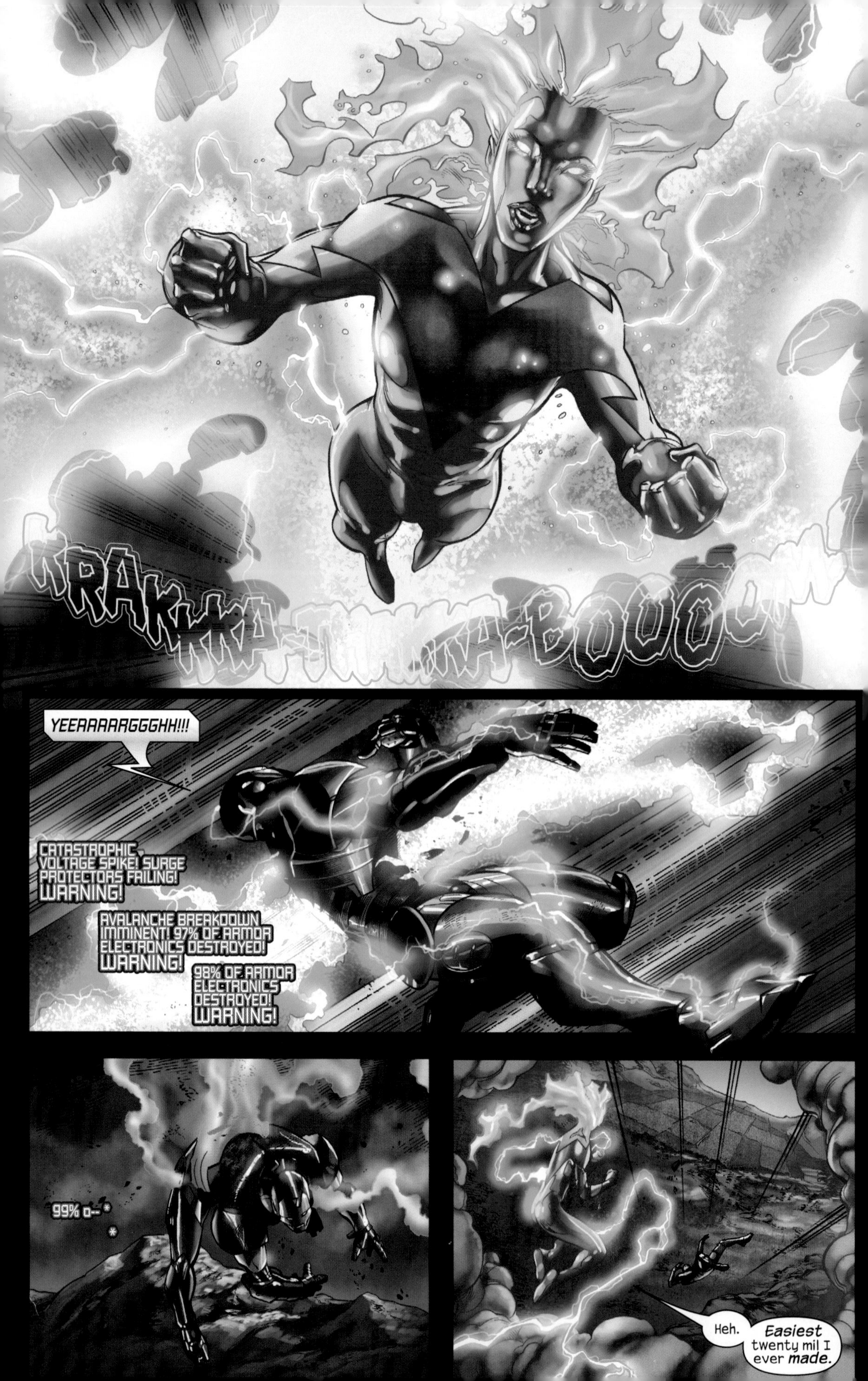
KRAKKA-THOOMKA-BOOOOOM!
YEEAAAAARGGGHH!!!
CATASTROPHIC VOLTAGE SPIKE! SURGE PROTECTORS FAILING! WARNING!
AVALANCHE BREAKDOWN IMMINENT! 97% OF ARMOR ELECTRONICS DESTROYED! WARNING!
98% OF ARMOR ELECTRONICS DESTROYED! WARNING!
99% O-- *
*
Heh.
Easiest twenty mil I ever made.

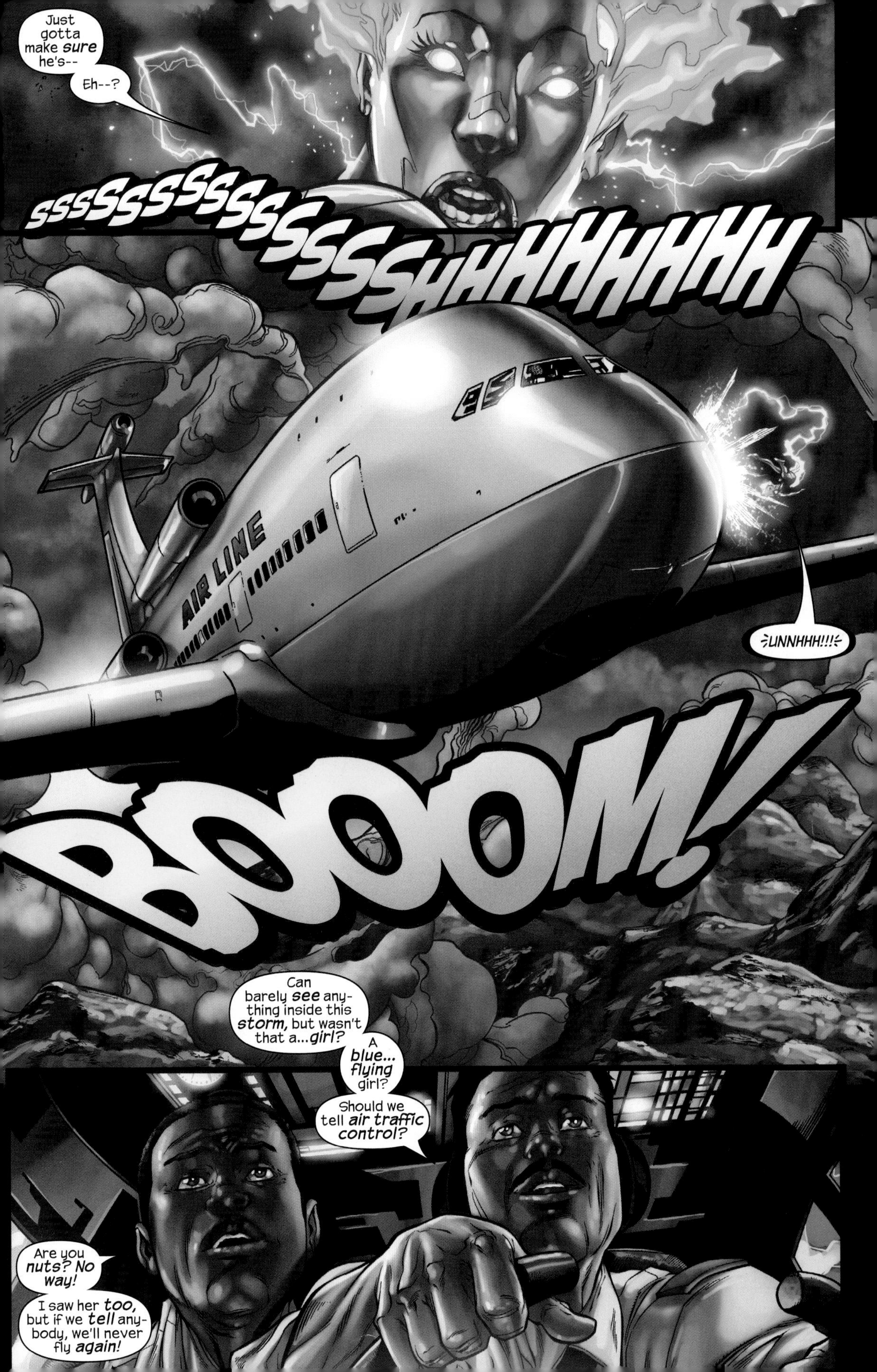
Just gotta make sure he's--
Eh--?
SSSSSSSSSSSSSHHHHHHHHHH
AIR LINE
UNNHHH!!!
BOOOM!
Can barely see anything inside this storm, but wasn't that a...girl?
A blue... flying girl?
Should we tell air traffic control?
Are you nuts? No way!
I saw her too, but if we tell anybody, we'll never fly again!

Isaiah!

Look!

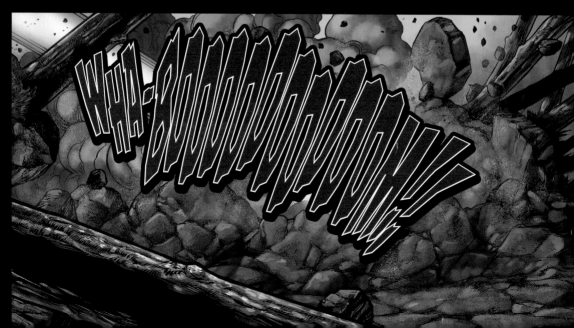

WHA-BOOOOOOOOOOOOKK!!

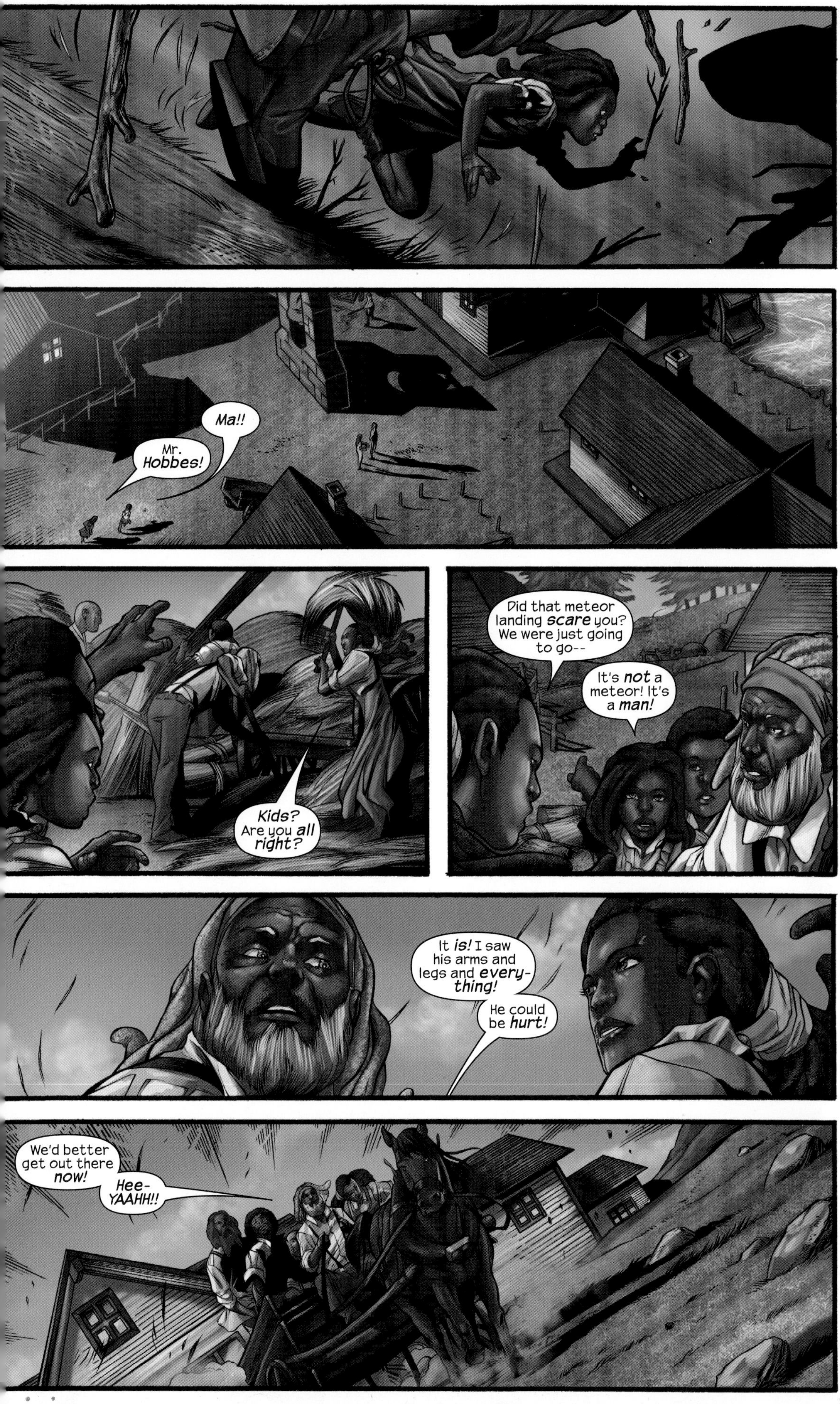
Ma!!
Mr. Hobbes!
Kids? Are you all right?
Did that meteor landing scare you? We were just going to go--
It's not a meteor! It's a man!
It is! I saw his arms and legs and every-thing!
He could be hurt!
We'd better get out there now!
Hee-YAAHH!!

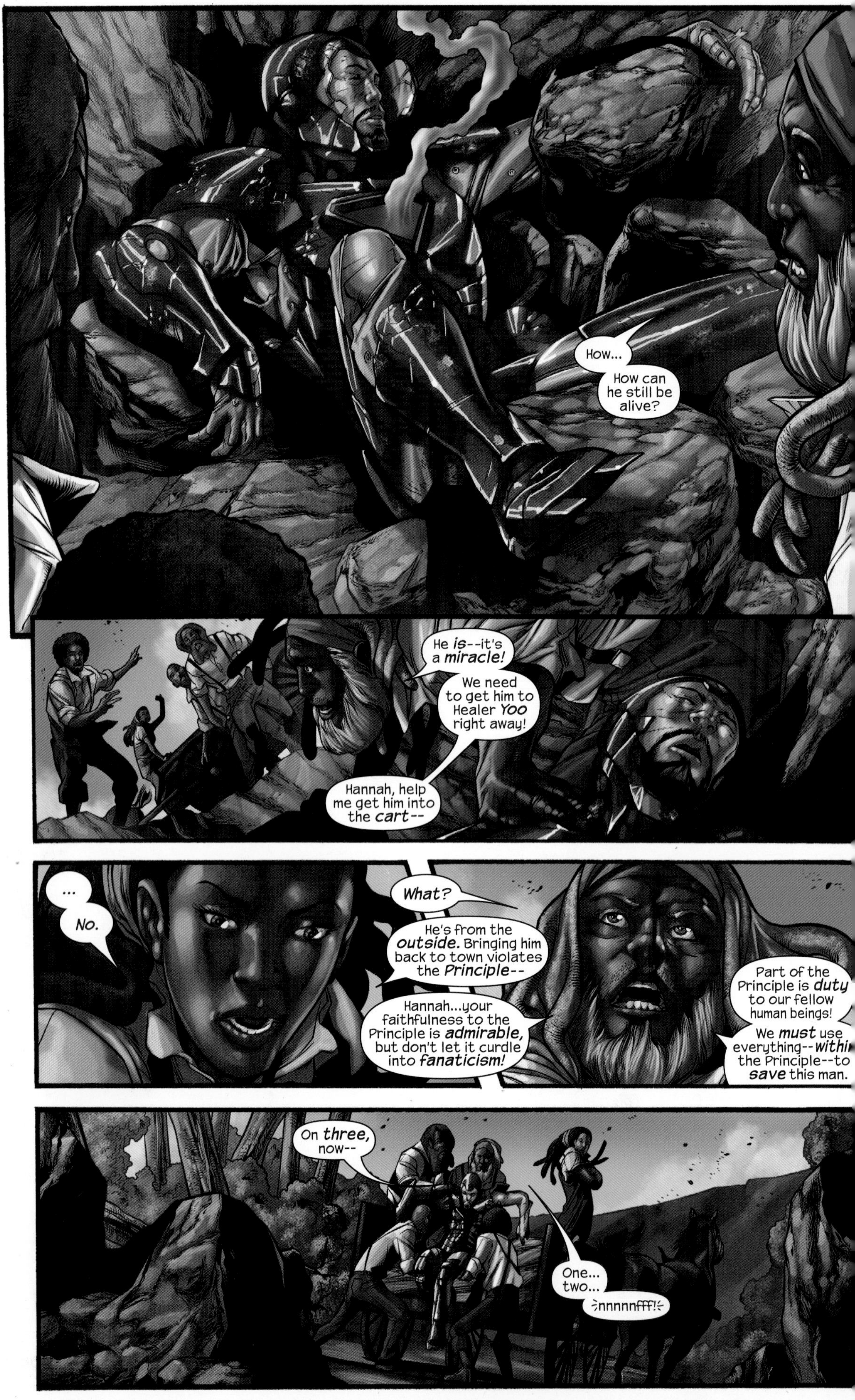

How...
How can he still be alive?
He is--it's a miracle!
We need to get him to Healer Yoo right away!
Hannah, help me get him into the cart--
...
No.
What?
He's from the outside. Bringing him back to town violates the Principle--
Hannah...your faithfulness to the Principle is admirable, but don't let it curdle into fanaticism!
Part of the Principle is duty to our fellow human beings!
We must use everything--withi the Principle--to save this man.
On three, now--
One... two...
nnnnnfff!

48 HOURS LATER...

Unnnnhh...

There, there. Don't move around too *much*, stranger.

We set your *broken leg* as best we could, but you're not out of the woods just *yet*.

Where am I? Who are--

Our village has *no name*. It's not even on a *map*. And that's the way we *like* it.

We've all... *opted out* of the modern world.

I used to be a *real estate developer*. I was pretty *good* at it, too. Jane *Yoo* here, was head of surgery at *Mt. Sinai*.

But we didn't want the *commercialism* and rampant *violence* of modern America to poison our *families*, so we've chosen to live here, in a *pacifist*, farming society, in the way that made our *ancestors* great.

I don't know how to repay you for what you've done--but--if I could ask *one* more thing--

My people are *worried* about me, I'm sure, and I'd like to *call* to let them know I'm all right--and so they can come *get* me--

I'm afraid that would be *impossible*. We have no *phones* of any kind--no Internet--no *television*. Technology is strictly *forbidden* here.

And the *thunderstorm* that passed through here last night made the road down the mountain too *rough* for somebody in your condition to go down on *horseback*.

You're stuck *here* until your body does some *healing*.

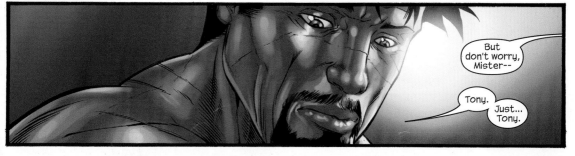

But don't worry, Mister--

Tony. Just... Tony.

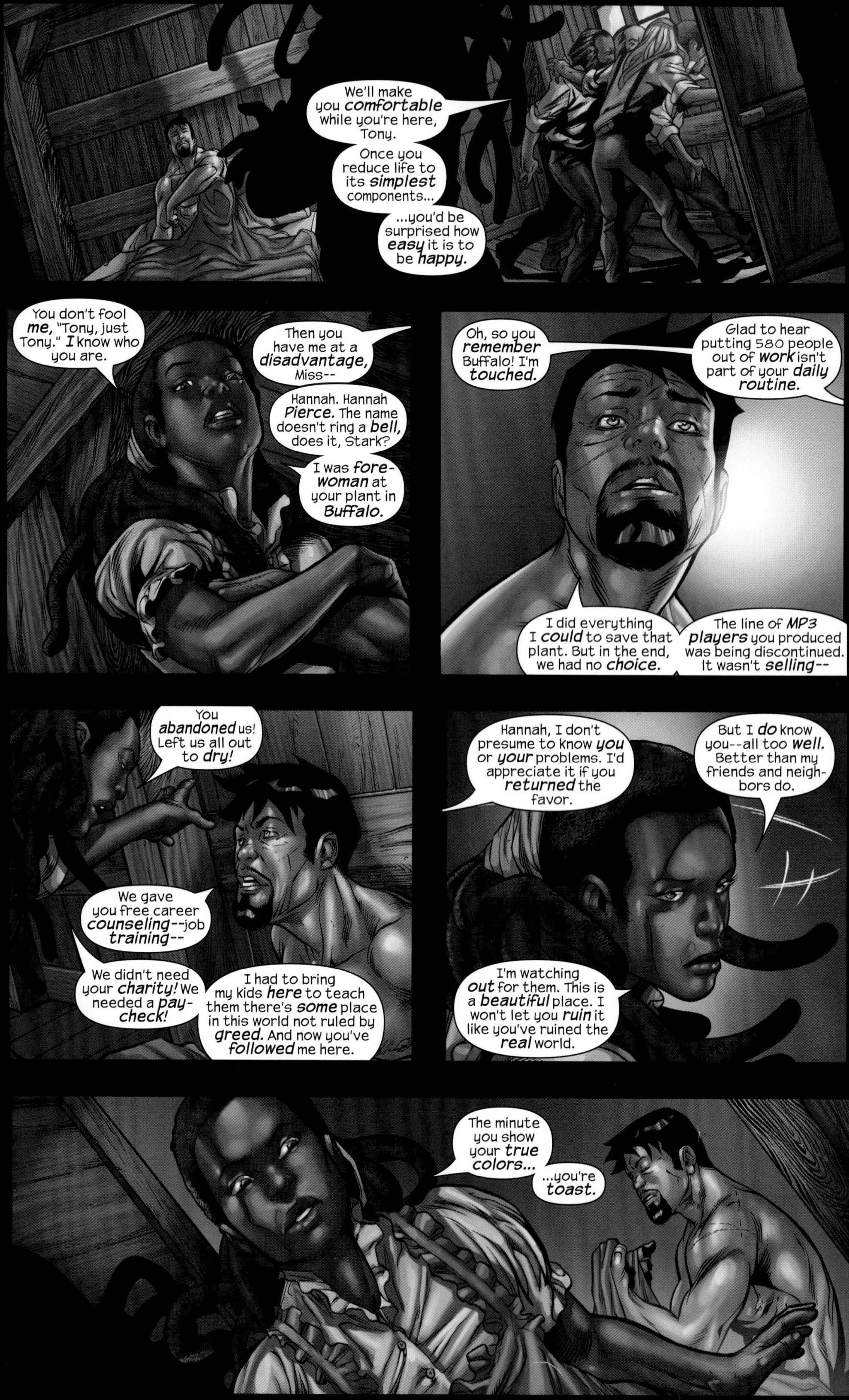
We'll make you comfortable while you're here, Tony.
Once you reduce life to its simplest components...
...you'd be surprised how easy it is to be happy.
You don't fool me, "Tony, just Tony." I know who you are.
Then you have me at a disadvantage, Miss--
Hannah. Hannah Pierce. The name doesn't ring a bell, does it, Stark?
I was fore-woman at your plant in Buffalo.
Oh, so you remember Buffalo! I'm touched.
Glad to hear putting 580 people out of work isn't part of your daily routine.
I did everything I could to save that plant. But in the end, we had no choice.
The line of MP3 players you produced was being discontinued. It wasn't selling--
You abandoned us! Left us all out to dry!
We gave you free career counseling--job training--
We didn't need your charity! We needed a pay-check!
I had to bring my kids here to teach them there's some place in this world not ruled by greed. And now you've followed me here.
Hannah, I don't presume to know you or your problems. I'd appreciate it if you returned the favor.
But I do know you--all too well. Better than my friends and neigh-bors do.
I'm watching out for them. This is a beautiful place. I won't let you ruin it like you've ruined the real world.
The minute you show your true colors...
...you're toast.

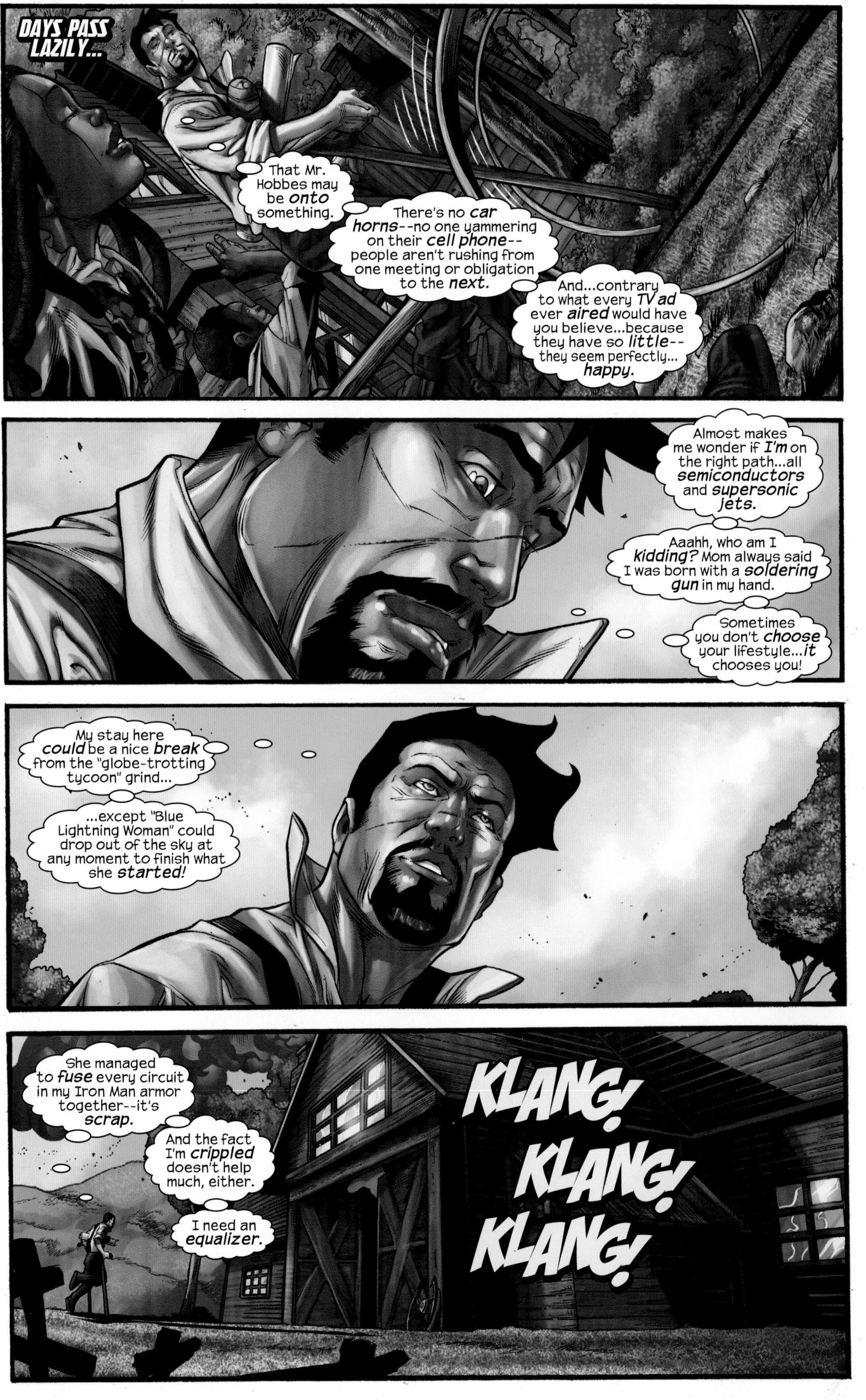
DAYS PASS LAZILY...
That Mr. Hobbes may be onto something.
There's no car horns--no one yammering on their cell phone--people aren't rushing from one meeting or obligation to the next.
And...contrary to what every TV ad ever aired would have you believe...because they have so little--they seem perfectly... happy.
Almost makes me wonder if I'm on the right path...all semiconductors and supersonic jets.
Aaahh, who am I kidding? Mom always said I was born with a soldering gun in my hand.
Sometimes you don't choose your lifestyle...it chooses you!
My stay here could be a nice break from the "globe-trotting tycoon" grind...
...except "Blue Lightning Woman" could drop out of the sky at any moment to finish what she started!
She managed to fuse every circuit in my Iron Man armor together--it's scrap.
And the fact I'm crippled doesn't help much, either.
I need an equalizer.
KLANG! KLANG! KLANG!

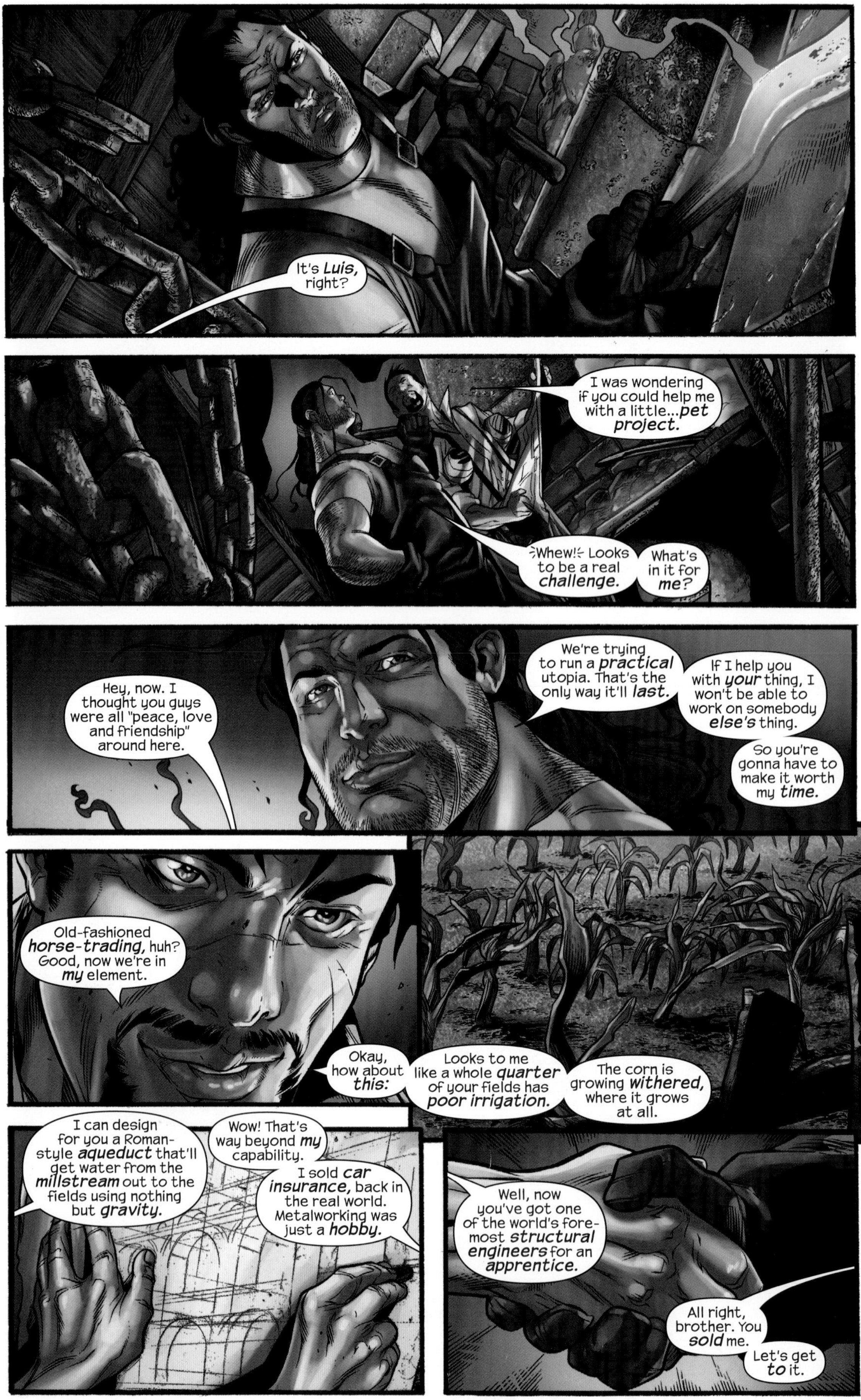

It's *Luis,* right?
I was wondering if you could help me with a little...*pet project.*
-Whew!- Looks to be a real *challenge.*
What's in it for *me?*
Hey, now. I thought you guys were all "peace, love and friendship" around here.
We're trying to run a *practical* utopia. That's the only way it'll *last.*
If I help you with *your* thing, I won't be able to work on somebody *else's* thing.
So you're gonna have to make it worth my *time.*
Old-fashioned *horse-trading,* huh? Good, now we're in *my* element.
Okay, how about *this:*
Looks to me like a whole *quarter* of your fields has *poor irrigation.*
The corn is growing *withered,* where it grows at all.
I can design for you a Roman-style *aqueduct* that'll get water from the *millstream* out to the fields using nothing but *gravity.*
Wow! That's way beyond *my* capability.
I sold *car insurance,* back in the real world. Metalworking was just a *hobby.*
Well, now you've got one of the world's fore-most *structural engineers* for an *apprentice.*
All right, brother. You *sold* me.
Let's get *to* it.

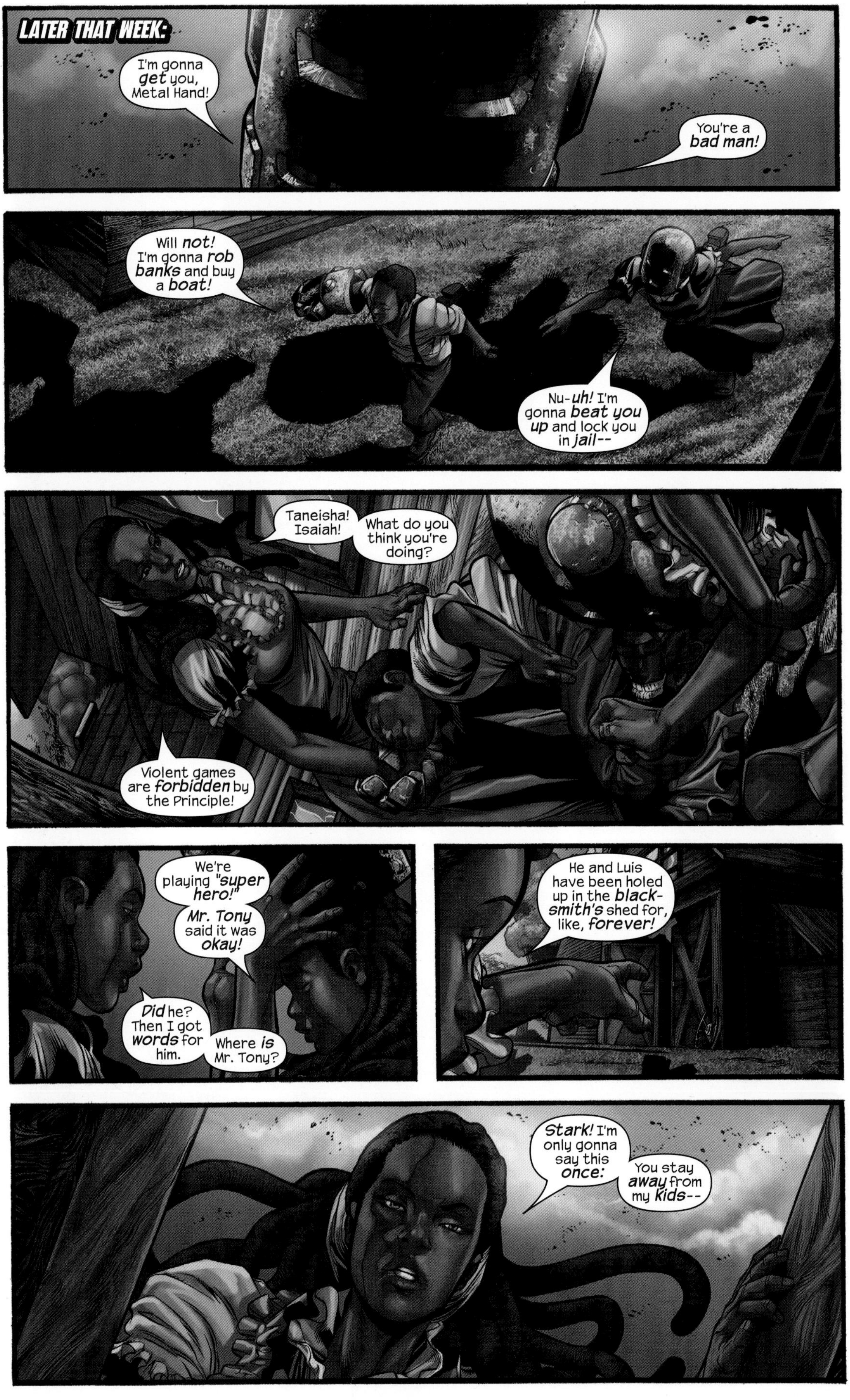

LATER THAT WEEK:
I'm gonna get you, Metal Hand!
You're a bad man!
Will not! I'm gonna rob banks and buy a boat!
Nu-uh! I'm gonna beat you up and lock you in jail--
Taneisha! Isaiah!
What do you think you're doing?
Violent games are forbidden by the Principle!
We're playing "super hero!" Mr. Tony said it was okay!
Did he? Then I got words for him.
Where is Mr. Tony?
He and Luis have been holed up in the black-smith's shed for, like, forever!
Stark! I'm only gonna say this once:
You stay away from my kids--

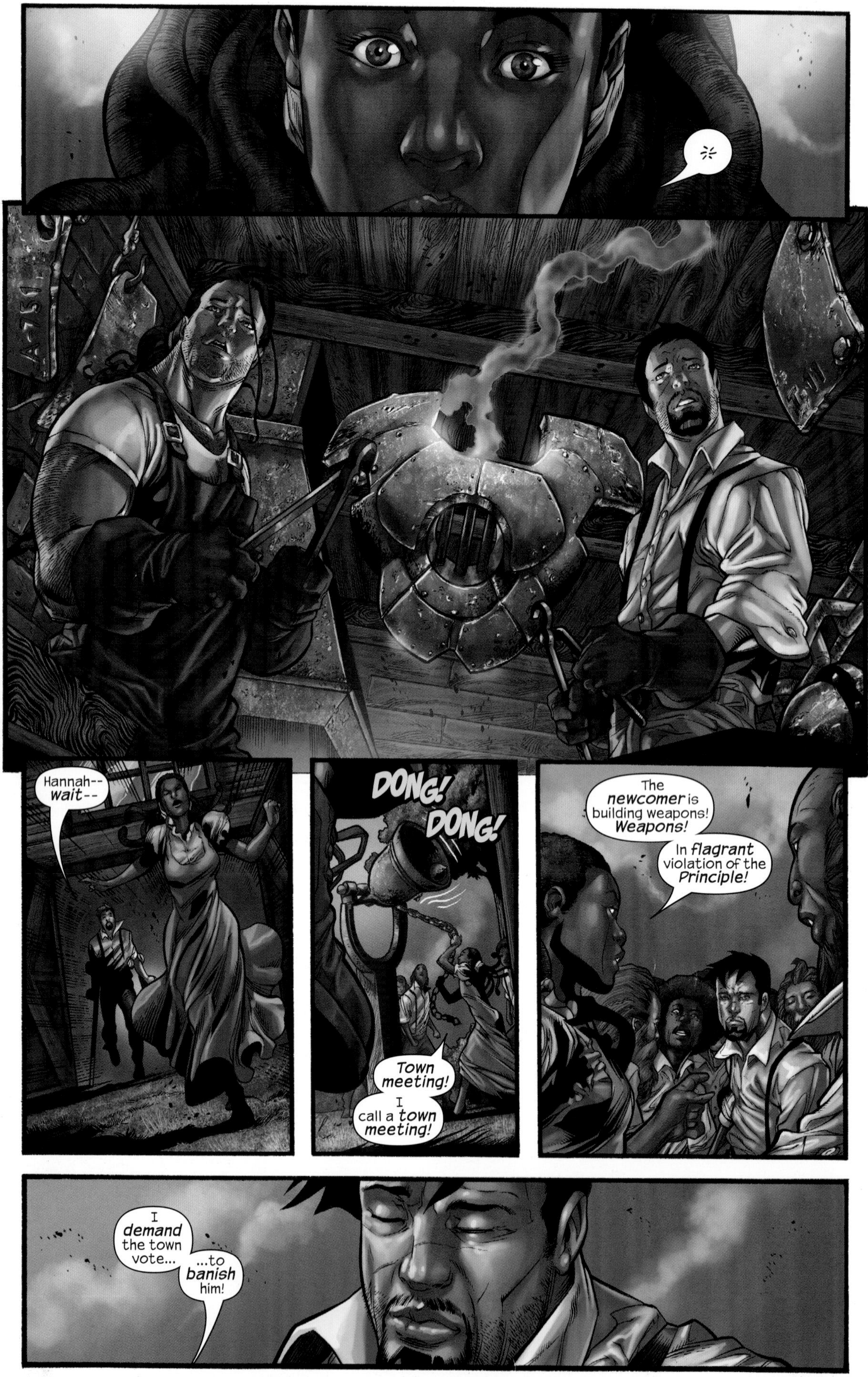

A-751
Hannah-- wait--
DONG! DONG!
Town meeting!
I call a town meeting!
The newcomer is building weapons! Weapons!
In flagrant violation of the Principle!
I demand the town vote...
...to banish him!

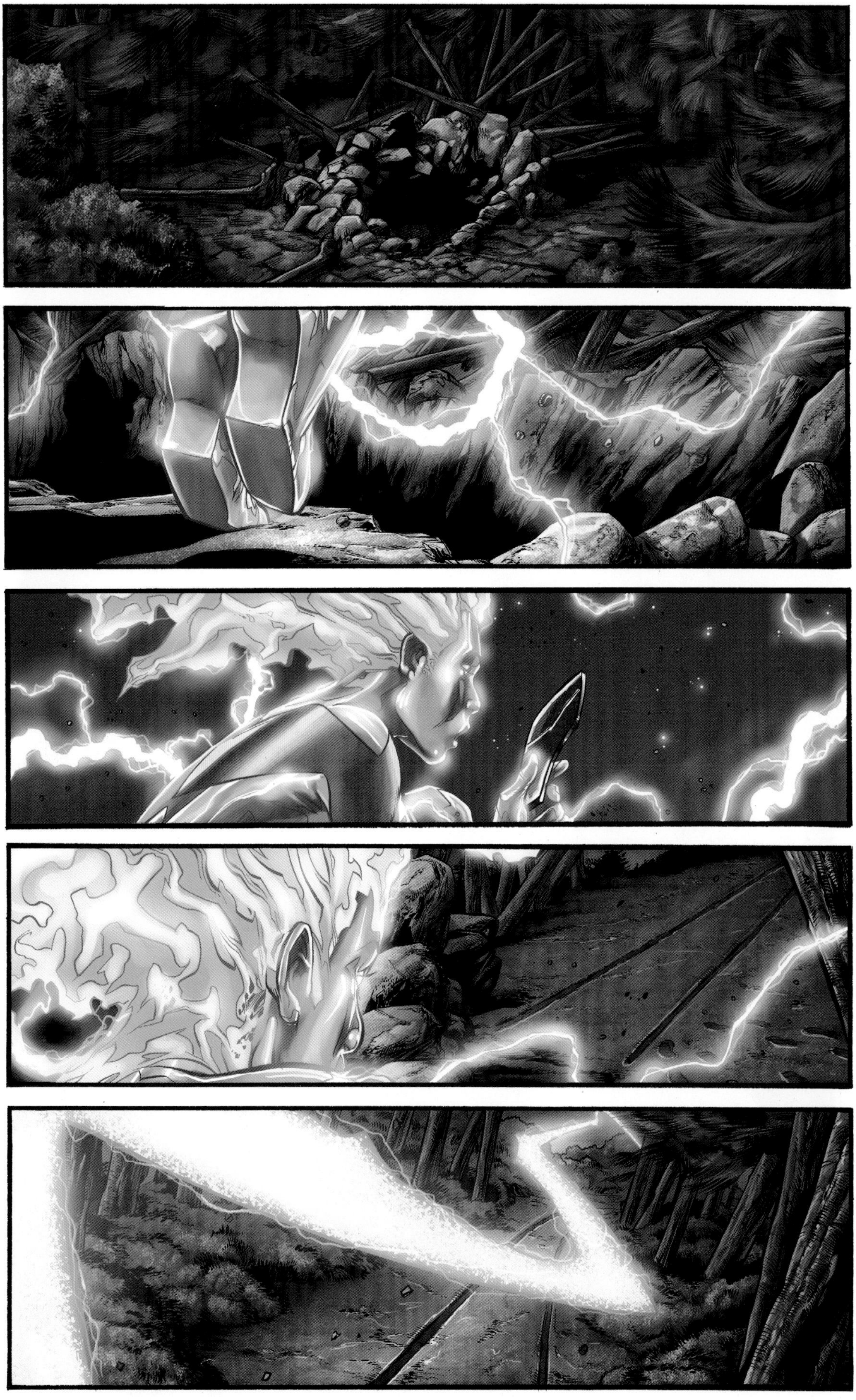

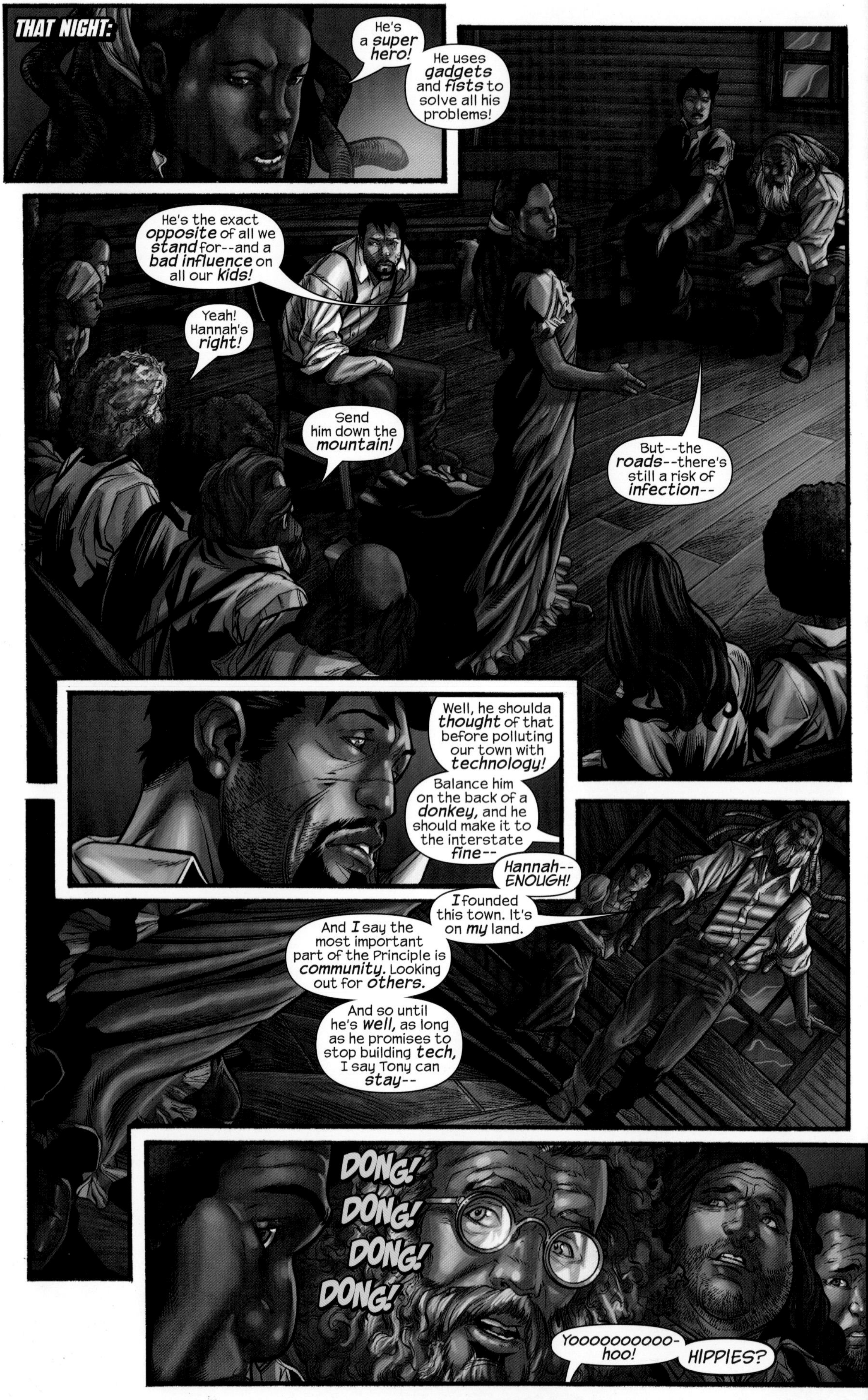

THAT NIGHT:
He's a super hero!
He uses gadgets and fists to solve all his problems!
He's the exact opposite of all we stand for--and a bad influence on all our kids!
Yeah! Hannah's right!
Send him down the mountain!
But--the roads--there's still a risk of infection--
Well, he shoulda thought of that before polluting our town with technology!
Balance him on the back of a donkey, and he should make it to the interstate fine--
Hannah--ENOUGH!
I founded this town. It's on my land.
And I say the most important part of the Principle is community. Looking out for others.
And so until he's well, as long as he promises to stop building tech, I say Tony can stay--
DONG!
DONG!
DONG!
DONG!
Yoooooooooo-hoo!
HIPPIES?

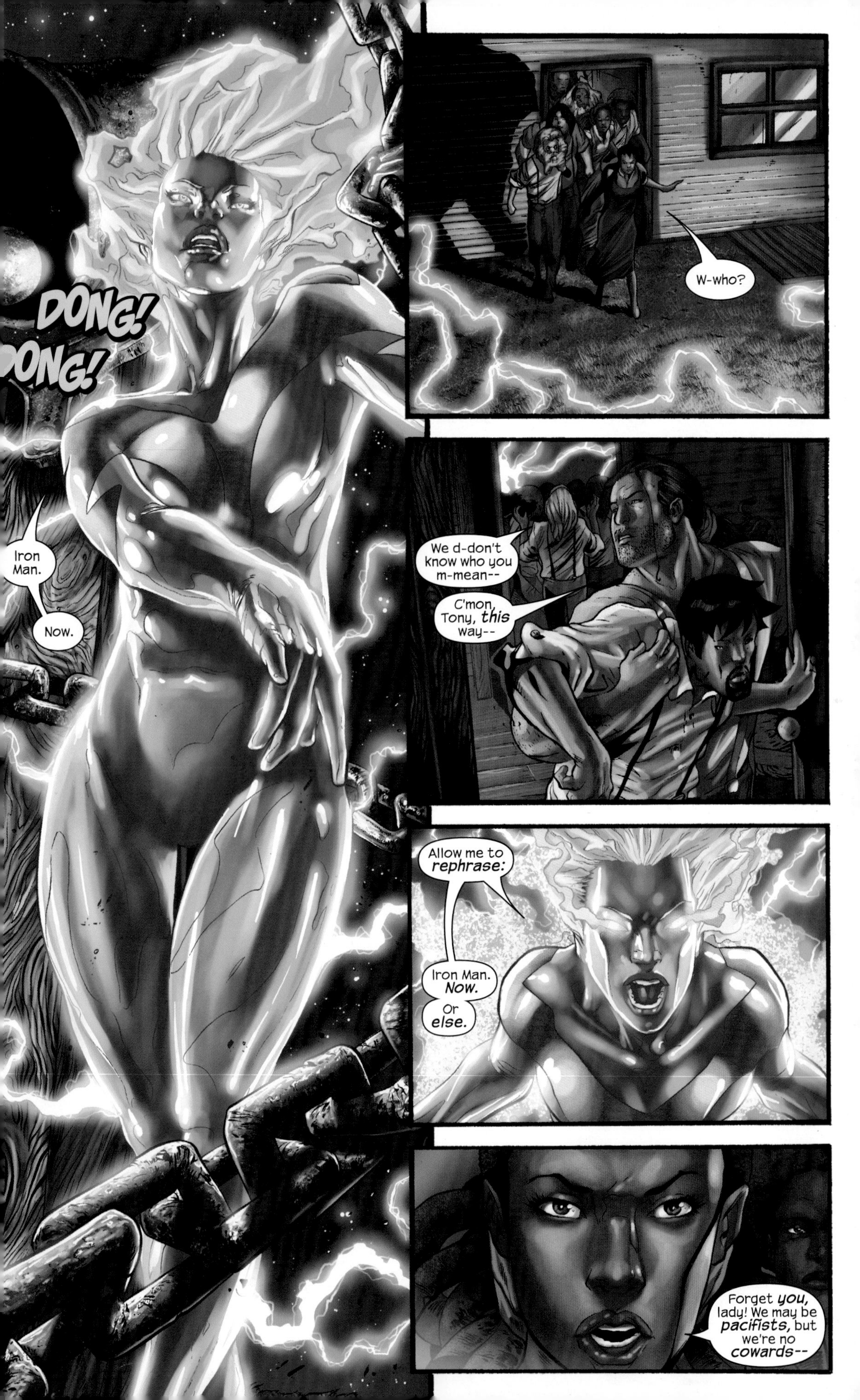
DONG!
DONG!
Iron Man.
Now.
W-who?
We d-don't know who you m-mean--
C'mon, Tony, this way--
Allow me to rephrase:
Iron Man. Now.
Or else.
Forget you, lady! We may be pacifists, but we're no cowards--

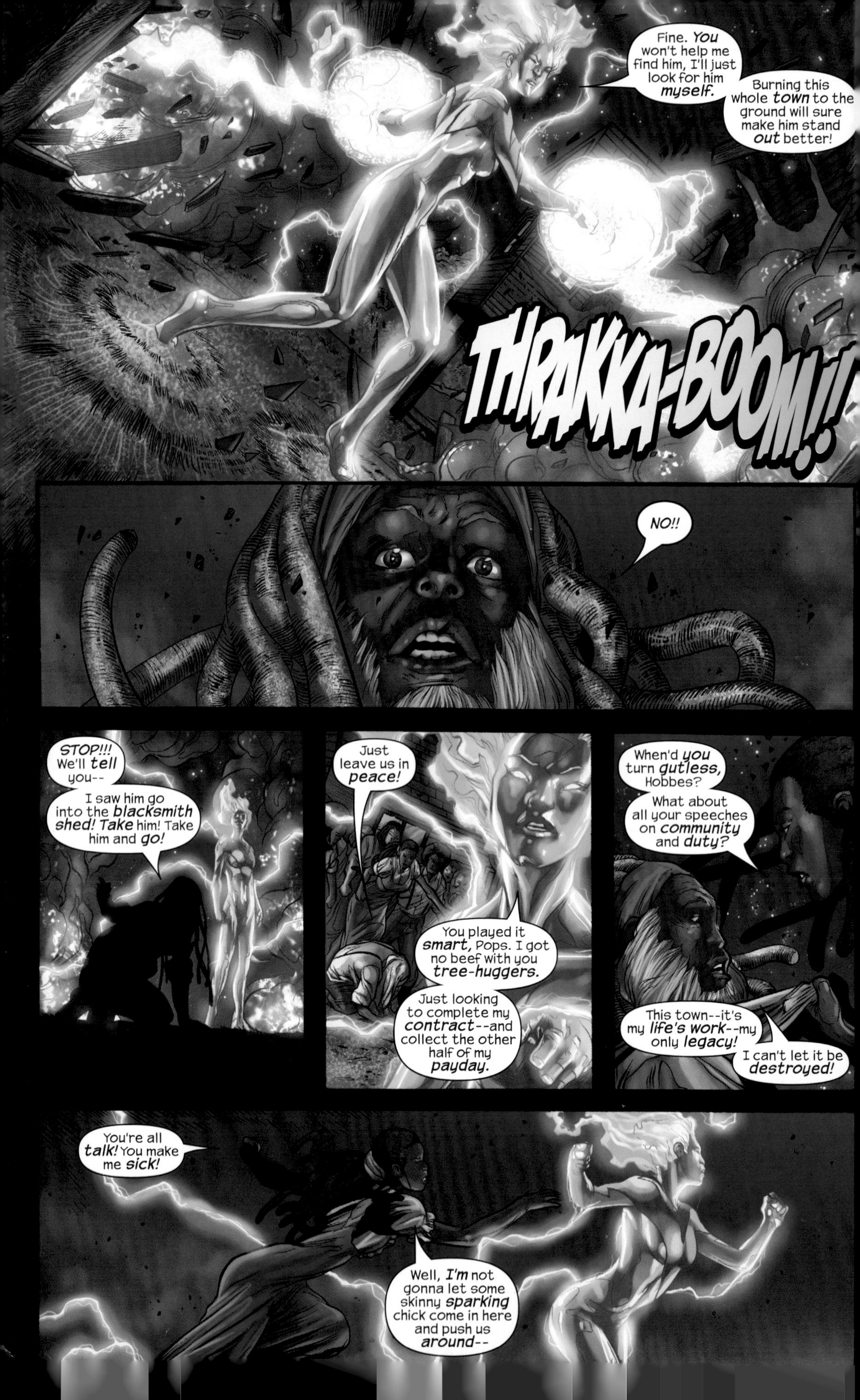

Fine. You won't help me find him, I'll just look for him myself.
Burning this whole town to the ground will sure make him stand out better!
THRAKKA-BOOM!!!
NO!!
STOP!!! We'll tell you--
I saw him go into the blacksmith shed! Take him! Take him and go!
Just leave us in peace!
You played it smart, Pops. I got no beef with you tree-huggers.
Just looking to complete my contract--and collect the other half of my payday.
When'd you turn gutless, Hobbes?
What about all your speeches on community and duty?
This town--it's my life's work--my only legacy!
I can't let it be destroyed!
You're all talk! You make me sick!
Well, I'm not gonna let some skinny sparking chick come in here and push us around--

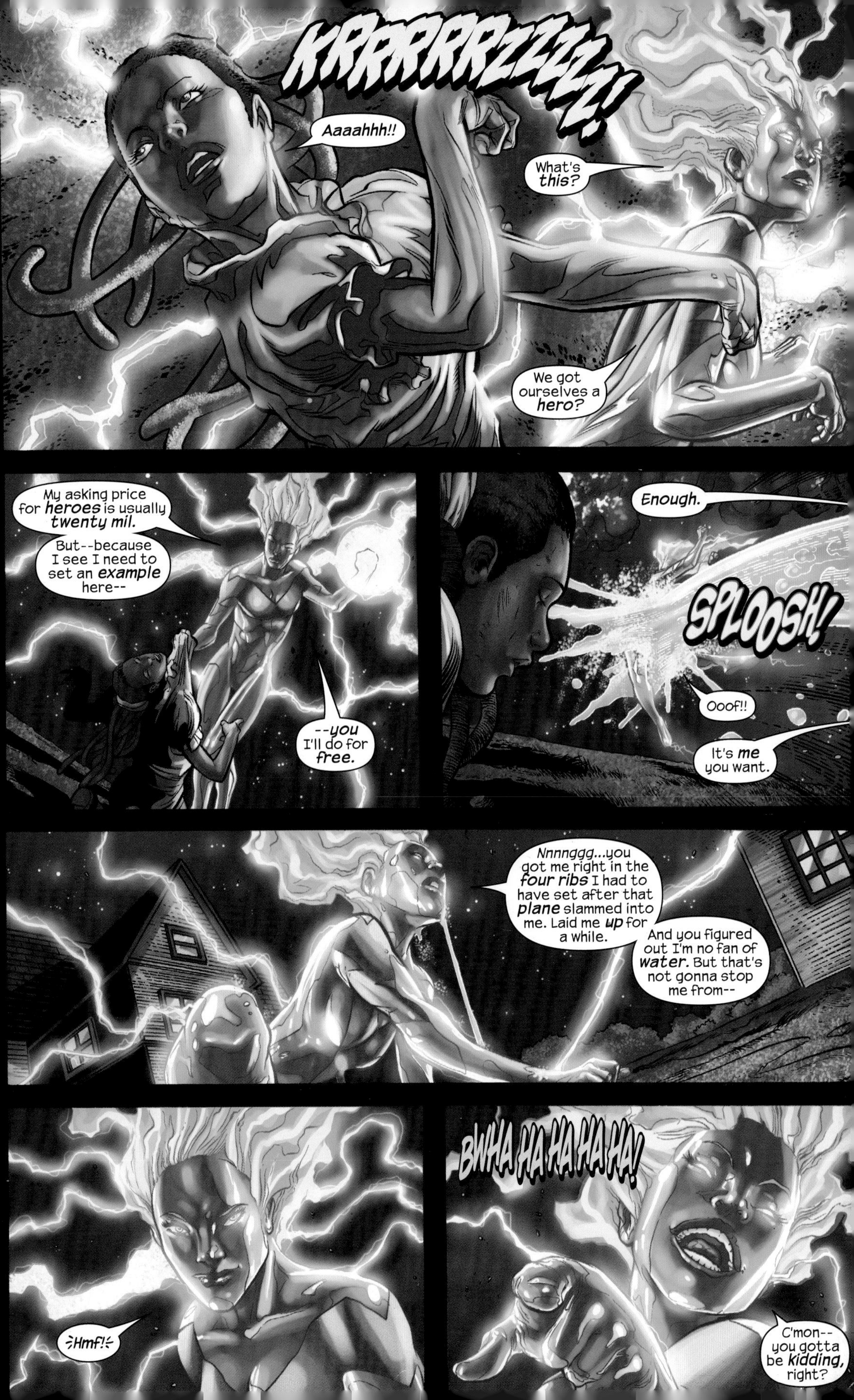
KRRRRRZZZZZ!
Aaaahhh!!
What's this?
We got ourselves a hero?
My asking price for heroes is usually twenty mil.
But--because I see I need to set an example here--
--you I'll do for free.
Enough.
SPLOOSH!
Ooof!!
It's me you want.
Nnnnggg...you got me right in the four ribs I had to have set after that plane slammed into me. Laid me up for a while.
And you figured out I'm no fan of water. But that's not gonna stop me from--
Hmf!
BWHA HA HA HA HA!
C'mon--you gotta be kidding, right?

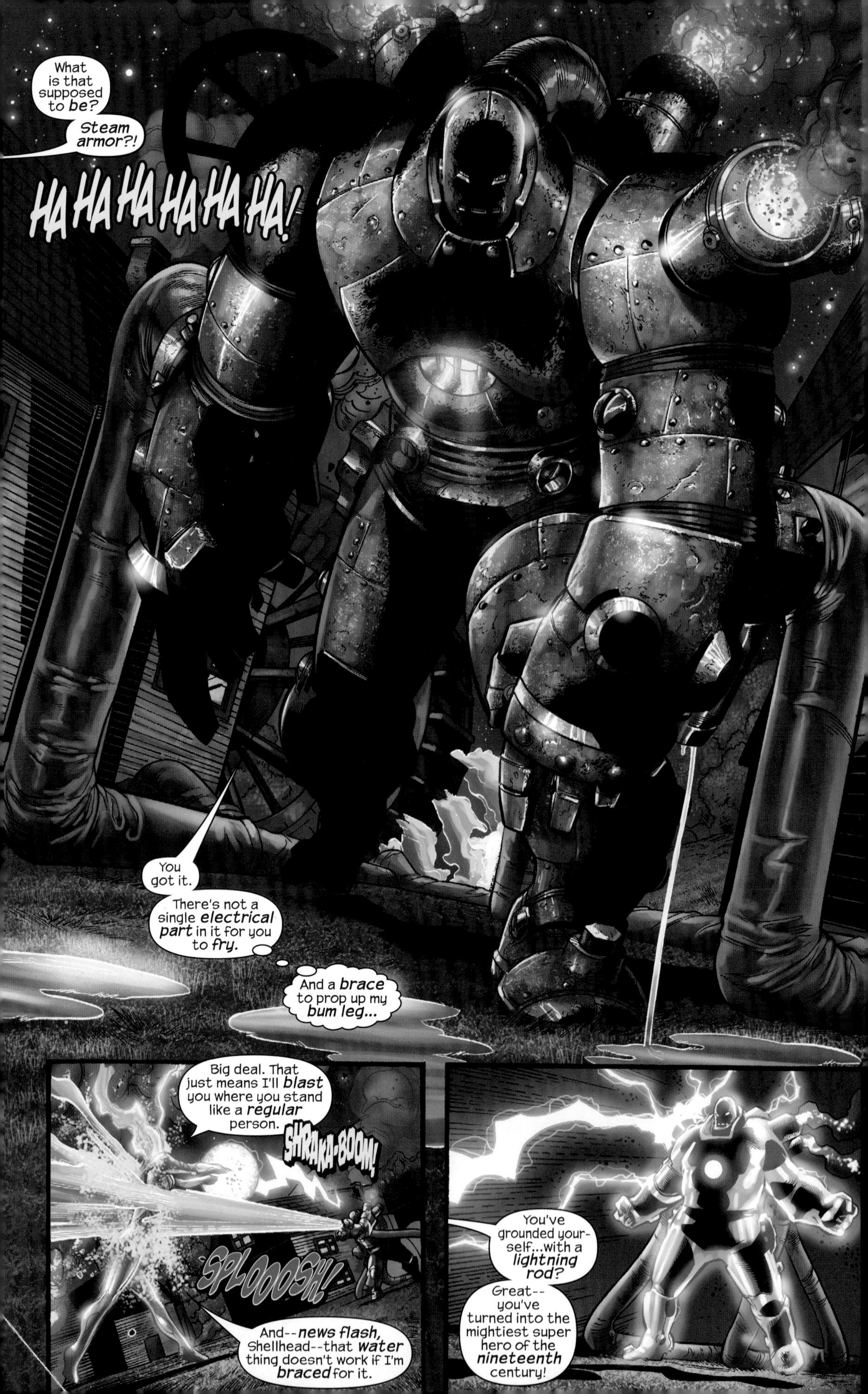
What is that supposed to be?
Steam armor?!
HA HA HA HA HA HA HA!
You got it.
There's not a single electrical part in it for you to fry.
And a brace to prop up my bum leg...
Big deal. That just means I'll blast you where you stand like a regular person.
SHRAKA-BOOM!
SPLOOOSH!
And--news flash, Shellhead--that water thing doesn't work if I'm braced for it.
You've grounded your-self...with a lightning rod?
Great--you've turned into the mightiest super hero of the nineteenth century!

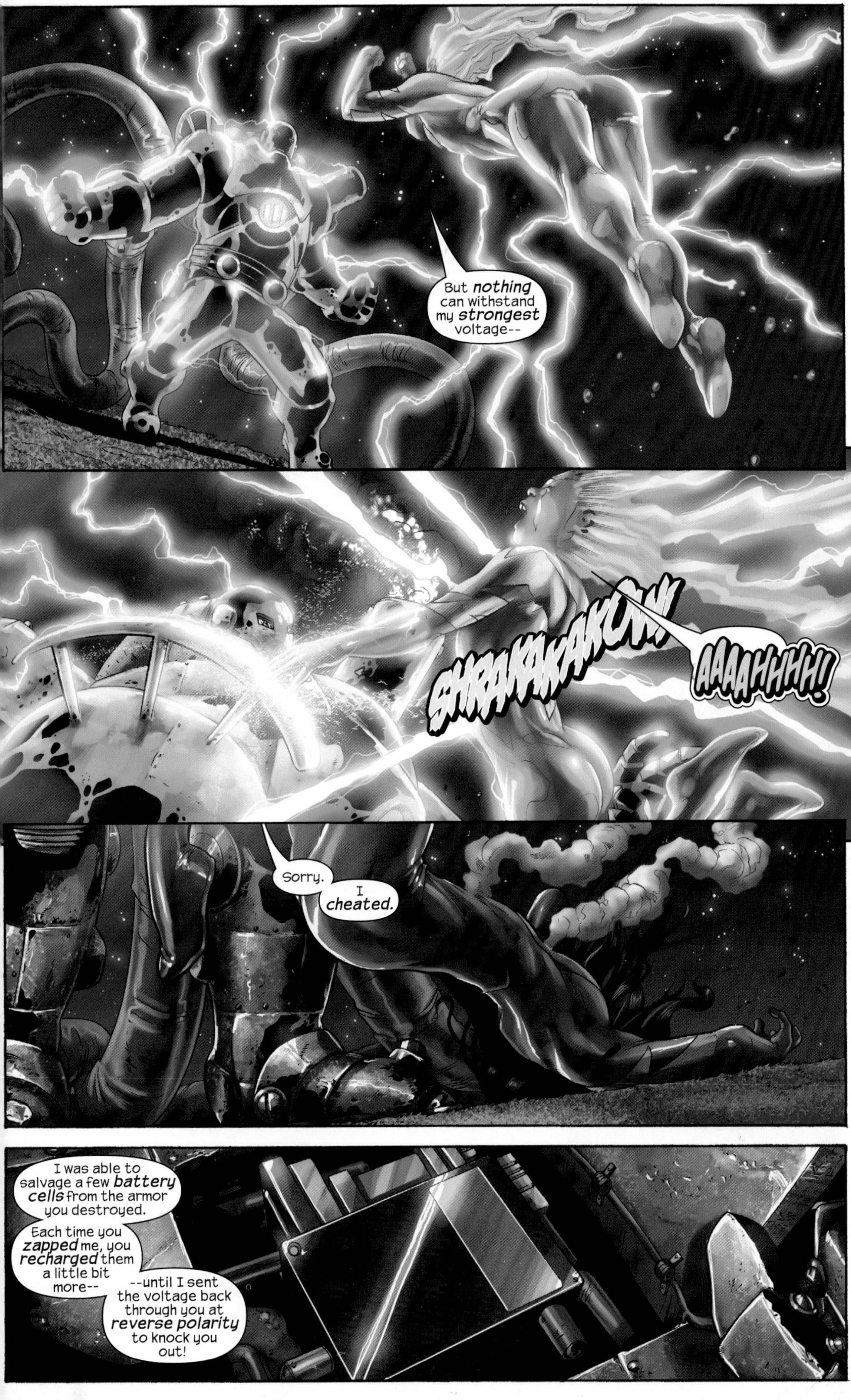

But nothing can withstand my strongest voltage--
SHRAKAKAKOW!
AAAAHHHH!
Sorry.
I cheated.
I was able to salvage a few battery cells from the armor you destroyed.
Each time you zapped me, you recharged them a little bit more--
--until I sent the voltage back through you at reverse polarity to knock you out!

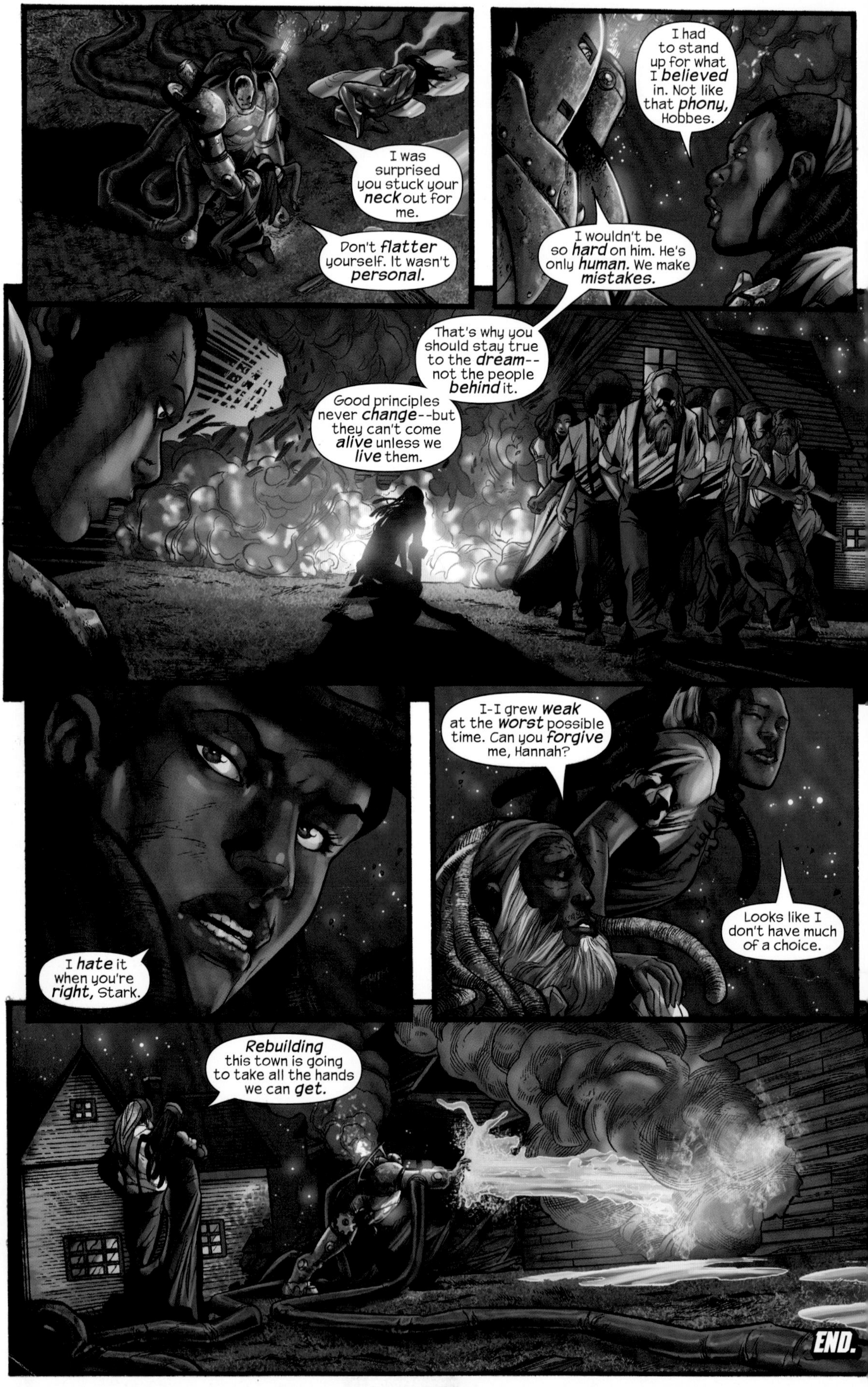
I was surprised you stuck your neck out for me.
Don't flatter yourself. It wasn't personal.
I had to stand up for what I believed in. Not like that phony, Hobbes.
I wouldn't be so hard on him. He's only human. We make mistakes.
That's why you should stay true to the dream--not the people behind it.
Good principles never change--but they can't come alive unless we live them.
I hate it when you're right, Stark.
I-I grew weak at the worst possible time. Can you forgive me, Hannah?
Looks like I don't have much of a choice.
Rebuilding this town is going to take all the hands we can get.
END.